To Luke, Layla
& Jackson

From Grandpa & Grandma Jan

Gloria Gaither

Cardinal Courage

Illustrations by
Christy Boyer

LIBRARY OF CONGRESS IN-PUBLICATION DATA

Gaither, Gloria
      Cardinal Courage/Gloria Gaither; edited by Gloria Gaither
      Illustrated by Christy Boyer
      Interior Designed by Susan Browne
      Cover by Chad Smith

First edition 2011

Copyright 2011 by Gloria Gaither
Published 2011 by Gaither Music Company
Printed in the USA
ISBN 978-0-9830486-1

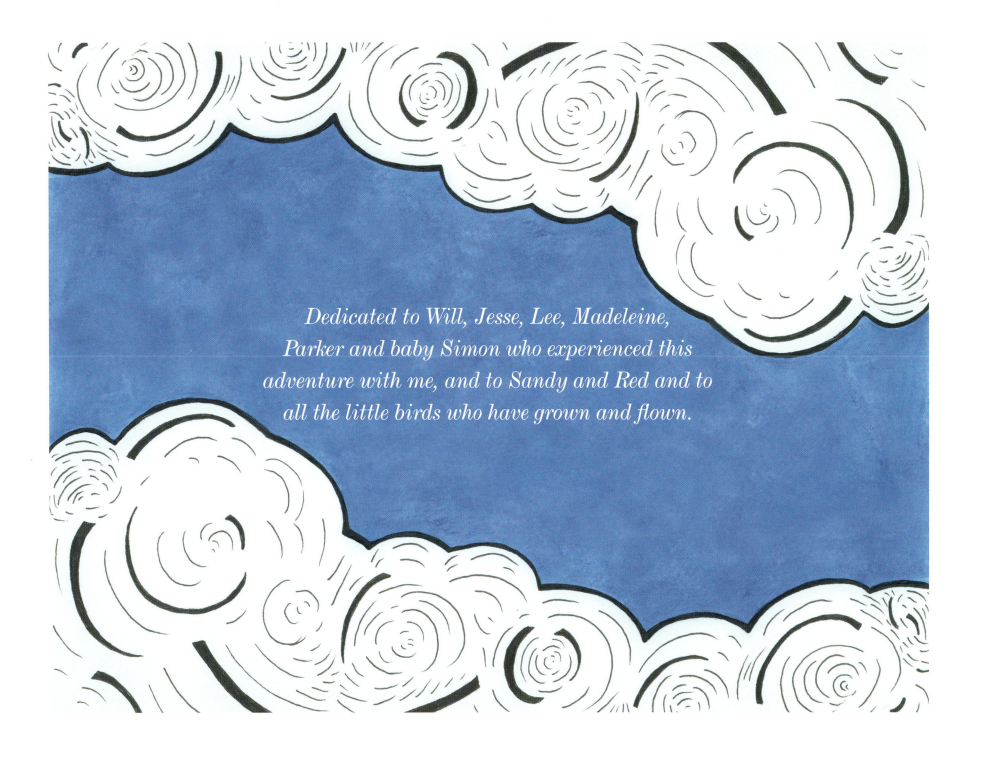

Dedicated to Will, Jesse, Lee, Madeleine, Parker and baby Simon who experienced this adventure with me, and to Sandy and Red and to all the little birds who have grown and flown.

Sandy Cardinal

was looking for a place to

build her nest

in the green pine yard
of Willowmere.

Back and forth she flew

looking for a spot where there would be shelter from the wind and where she could watch for danger without leaving her eggs.

It was Red who actually located the hidden spot in the clematis vine growing thick on the wire lattice between the grape arbor and the prickly pyracantha.

"Hey, Sandy!" he chirped.
"Come check this out."

Sandy flew over from the cedar hedge where she had been searching.

"This is incredible!"
she exclaimed when she saw Red's find.
"Perfect in every way!"

Red's chest
swelled with pride
that she was so pleased.

"I'll help you get the **big** stuff," he told her.

"You look for **small** twigs and soft lining."

Off they both flew
to find the perfect materials
for their soon-coming

family.

Now, the house at Willowmere was a big colonial house with huge white pillars.

It sat on top of a green hill with a tree-filled lawn sweeping down toward a white trellis covered with pink roses.

Beyond the fence, the trellis, and the roses was Gaither's pond. This is where the children fished and the whole family had picnics under the weeping willow trees.

The cardinals weren't the only family building nests this time of year.

The black swan and the Canadian geese were busy carrying sticks for nests and so were the mallards and the colorful wood ducks.

Like all good parents, the waterfowl were each searching for a place where their babies would be sheltered and safe.

The family on the hilltop

was busy, too. Their home had been
built for close to forty years, and

it was time for new insulation and siding

to keep the family inside
warm in the winter when
the snows came and the
North Wind blew.

All around the yard
lay piles of
old siding
boards and
discarded
insulation.

"How lucky can we be?"

thought Sandy Cardinal.

"These puffs of insulation will be great for our house too."

She pulled a loose piece of lining from the siding and

carried it to their nest
in the clematis vines.

Red had already finished
the framework for their nest

and had anchored it solidly between the strong vines

and the wire lattice.

Skillfully, Sandy wove the soft insulation in between the sticks, packing it into place with her strong triangular beak.

She filled in all the spaces so that no air could blow through.

Back and forth she flew
time and time again,
bringing soft lining to
pack the nest.

That Sunday morning
she was so intent on her work,
she hadn't noticed the car that
had come in the wee hours . . .
or the couple that had come up the walk
under the grape arbor with travel bags.

In fact, not until a light switched on in the window behind the lattice and a woman began moving around in the kitchen behind it, did Sandy realize that

their nest was looking right into the face of the woman making coffee at the kitchen sink!

Sandy felt panic rising in her throat.

The nest was almost finished! What should they do?

What they thought was the safest place on the hill had suddenly become the most dangerous!

"Red! What shall we do?"

she shrieked in alarm as she flew to the barn-shaped birdfeeder by the gas lamppost.

Red came flying to her side as fast as he could.

31

"The people! They will see us. We can't trust this place now. Whatever shall we do?"

"Now Sandy, calm down." Red's tone was steady and sensible.

"They may not bother us. Don't leap to conclusions."

"But, but…what if they eat our eggs; or capture our babies? What if they have a cat? What if they tear our nest down? What if…"

"Enough 'what ifs!'"
Red interrupted.

"Let's take it slowly and be alert.

Things may not be as bad as you think."

All day long,
Sandy and Red carefully
put the finishing
touches on their nest.

And all day long
people went in and out
the door under
the grape arbor.

Sometimes

a face at the sink on the other side of the window would **frighten Sandy off her nest.**

But she would always come back.
She had to.

She could feel the time was close that she would
begin laying her eggs. The feathers on her breast
were starting to be loose, and as they loosened,
she pulled them out to
line the nest with the final layer
—the down that would help
keep her eggs warm.

Four days later, the light
in the window never came on.
All day long there was no
movement in the house.

"Maybe they're gone." Sandy said to Red when he came to bring her some black sunflower seeds to eat.

"Maybe." Red answered. "At any rate, no one has bothered us."

"Yes, you're right," she answered. "But it scares me every time I wake up to find someone staring me in the face."

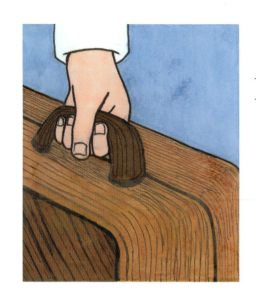

For two more days no one moved inside the house. Then, just like the week before, the two people came up the walk with their suitcases very early on Sunday morning.

The light went on over the clematis-covered window, and a woman started running water to make coffee.

By now the warm eggs under Sandy's breast made her stay very still, even though her heart was beating hard and the instinct to fly away was almost more than she could bear.

The woman disappeared for a while,
and then she returned to the window.

She climbed up
on a chair and began
taping a large piece of
green paper
to the window.

This time,
Sandy flew to the
bird feeder to watch.
Red flew in from the
white pine over the garden
swing to watch with her.

The green paper screen didn't seem
threatening at all to Red and Sandy.

Green was the color they were
used to having around them.

The leaves of the trees were green.

The grasses where they gathered seeds to eat were green. Their cozy clematis vine was green.

With the green paper in place Sandy could hardly tell when someone was moving around the kitchen.

No one watched her anymore as she sat on her nest.

Slowly, carefully,
she grew comfortable on her nest.

She began to feel as if the people in the house were her friends. When the children of the house peeked around the green screen, she didn't mind anymore.

No one tried to harm her.

One day
when
a long yellow cat
came up the
driveway,
the children
chased him away.

The woman poured
yummy sunflower
seeds
into the birdfeeder everyday
so Sandy could grab a quick lunch without having
to leave her nest long enough to let her eggs cool.

Fresh, clean water
always filled the birdbath
in the iris garden.

Sandy and Red talked about
living so close to the people house.

They decided that maybe
people weren't always
something to be afraid of.
Maybe some people
wanted to
help birds feel safe?

One morning Sandy flew to the feeder
for a quick breakfast.

When she got back,
she noticed a crack
in one of her eggs.

She knew soon there would be a peeping sound.

The eggs would split open,
and she would be a mother!

Sure enough, the next day
four naked baby birds, tiny and helpless,
their eyes still sealed shut,
were chirping with hunger.

"Feed me! Feed me!"
they yelled all morning.
Back and forth, back and forth,
Sandy and Red both flew stuffing food first in one
wide-open mouth and then the other.

How quickly their babies grew!

Soon, wispy little feathers popped out of their naked bodies. Then real, fuzzy feathers began to grow. As the babies grew bigger and bigger, the nest seemed to grow smaller and smaller.

They could barely fit in the nest, and at night Sandy had to sit half in and half out to cover them and keep the babies warm 'til morning.

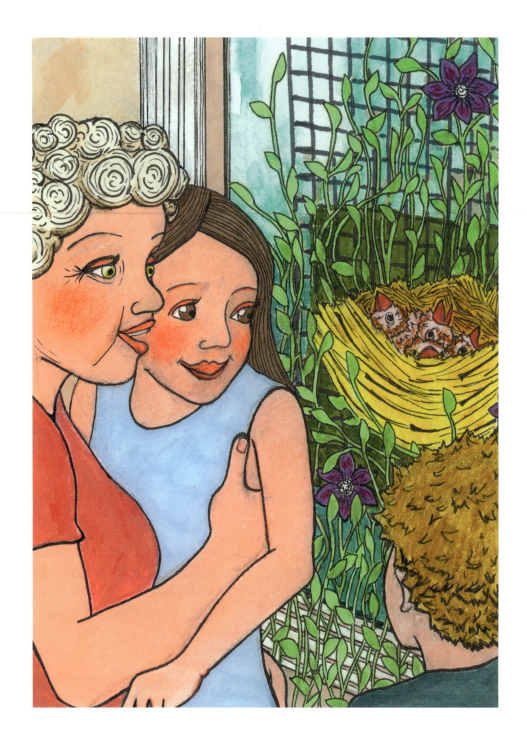

One by one,
the grandmother

—the woman who Red and Sandy
had seen working in the kitchen,

held the children up to see
the open mouths and
fuzzy bodies that
wiggled in the nest.

One Tuesday two of the house people's grandsons, named Jesse and Will, came to play on the hillside yard of the house at Willowmere.

Soon Lee and Madeleine came, too; then little Parker came and baby Simon.

And Sandy didn't mind one bit
having the children peep around
the green screen at her beautiful babies.
In fact, she couldn't help feeling a little proud
when she heard the children say,

"Oh! Aren't they cute!"

It was Auburn **who first adventured up onto the side of the nest** and from there to the metal edge of the lattice.

Like any good mother would,
Sandy yelled at him.

"You be careful, Auburn,"

she chirped from the nearby birdfeeder.

"You'll fall off of there backwards and crack your little cranium!"

But in her heart,
she was glad he had tried and proud that
he balanced himself so well. And, like a good bird,
he obeyed his mother and hopped back down into the nest.

Throughout the day, though, he and his
brother and sisters flapped their tiny wings
and stretched up tall on their legs.

Something inside them
seemed to be calling them
to stand tall, to hop, and to fly.

The children in the house kept peeking at the birds.

Whenever the birds hopped up on the trellis and flapped their wings, the children on the other side of the window clapped their hands and cheered!

On Thursday morning the woman
came to the window.
She started the coffee then
peeked around the green screen
to check on the birds.

There were no hungry beaks
open for food.
There were no fuzzy wings flapping.
There were no eager birds
hopping up onto the trellis.

The woman dialed the phone
on the wall by the sink.

"They've flown! Jesse,"
she said excitedly.
"The birds have flown.
The nest is empty."

It wasn't long until the children came.

Together the woman and the children peeled the green paper from the window.

The woman looked at the children.
She smiled a strange smile at them.

One by one, they looked into the empty nest.

Then, satisfied with their part in the adventure, they ran out the front door and down the hillside to the tall slide and swings where their parents, too, had once played away summer days.

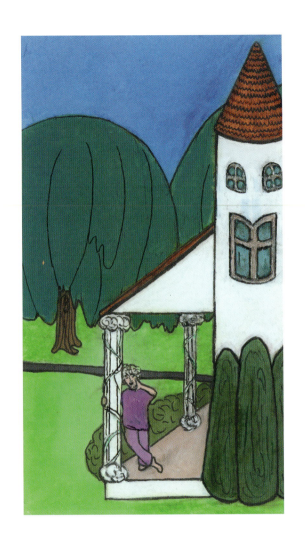

The woman watched them
from her front porch.

"You kids
be careful
when you climb
that slide,"
she said.

"You'll **fall** and **crack your craniums!**"

The author with the children
who lived this story—
Jesse, Will, Lee
and Madeleine . . .

. . . and Baby Simon.

The real Willowmere
overlooking Gaither's Pond

ABOUT THE AUTHOR

GLORIA GAITHER is an author, lyricist and a full time grandmother and lives on the hill in the house called Willowmere overlooking Gaither's Pond in Alexandria, Indiana. She has written over 40 books for both adults and children and lyrics to over 700 songs.

ABOUT THE ILLUSTRATOR

CHRISTY SPAULDING BOYER graduated from Anderson University with a B.A. in Graphic Design. For the past several years she has focused on Painting and Illustration. She lives with her husband and three sons in the Midwest. You can see more of her work at *www.hometownartroom.squarespace.com.*

Cardinals

The male is a bright red bird with a pointed crest on the top of his head. The female is mostly buff brown in color with some red on her head, wings, and tail. Both have small black masks on their faces that surround the bill and eyes. About 8 1/2 inches long.

While a somewhat secretive bird while nesting, you may still be able to watch from a distance. If she feels threatened, the female bird will abandon her nest building and find a new location. Always watch from a distance. The female builds the nest while the male keeps a close eye on her and the surrounding territory for predators and other males.

The nest is made up of twigs, bark strips, vines leaves, rootlets, paper, and lined with vines, grass and hair. You can find the nest placed in dense shrubbery or among branches of small trees, generally 1-15 feet above ground. There will be 2-5 buff-white eggs with dark marks. The female incubates the eggs for 12- 13 days and the young leave the nest in 9-11 days after hatching.

The female will be the only one incubating the eggs. The male's duty during this time is to feed her on the nest and protect their territory from intruders. Once the young hatch, both will feed them.

Typically, Northern Cardinal pairs remain together the whole year. Pairs often stay mated until one dies at which time the surviving mate will look for another partner.

Clematis

(KLEM-a-tis) is a member of the Ranunculaceae (buttercup) family. The word is from the Greek and means "vine." There are 250 species and numerous garden hybrids. There is great variety in flower form, color, bloom season, foliage effect and plant height. Leaves are opposite on the stem and mostly compound with three to five leaflets. The leaf stalk twines like a tendril and is responsible for giving the plant support. The flowers are showy, having four (sometimes five to eight) petal-like sepals in numerous colors and shades. Some other names for Clematis are traveler's joy, old man's beard, leather flower, vase vine and virgin's bower.